J
Dobkin   Dobkin, Bonnie
ER   Just a little
          different

DATE DUE		
MAR - 6 1995	JAN 2 5 1999	
APR 1 2 1995	JAN 2 7 1999	
AUG 2 2 1995	MAR 1 8 1999	
OCT 1 8 1995		
JUL 1 5 1997	MAY _ 3 1999	
MAR - 6 1998	JUN 1 4 1999	
APR - 8 1998	JUL 2 8 1999	
JUL 1 0 1998	AUG 1 1 1999	
AUG - 4 1998	DEC - 1 1999	
OCT 1 3 1998	JUN 7 2000	
DEC 2 3 1998	AUG - 7 2000	

A ROOKIE READER®

JUST A LITTLE DIFFERENT

By Bonnie Dobkin

Illustrated by Keith Neely

Prepared under the direction of Robert Hillerich, Ph.D.

CHILDRENS PRESS®

CHICAGO

For the world's best Mom and Dad.

Library of Congress Cataloging-in-Publication Data

Dobkin, Bonnie.
    Just a little different / by Bonnie Dobkin ; illustrated
by Keith Neely.
        p.   cm. — (A Rookie reader)
    Summary: A child relates how he and his best friend,
who is in a wheelchair, are both alike and different.
    ISBN 0-516-02018-8
    [1. Physically handicapped—Fiction. 2. Friendship—
Fiction.] I. Neely, Keith, ill. II. Title. III. Series.
PZ7.D656Ju   1993
[E]—dc20   93-13024
                                                      CIP
                                                       AC

This is Josh.

He's a lot like me.

That's why he's my
very best friend.

Of course, he is
a little different.

Josh loves school—
just like me.

He plays catch—
just like me.

He loves monster movies—
just like me.

And we listen to the same music.

But . . . I walk.

Josh zooms.

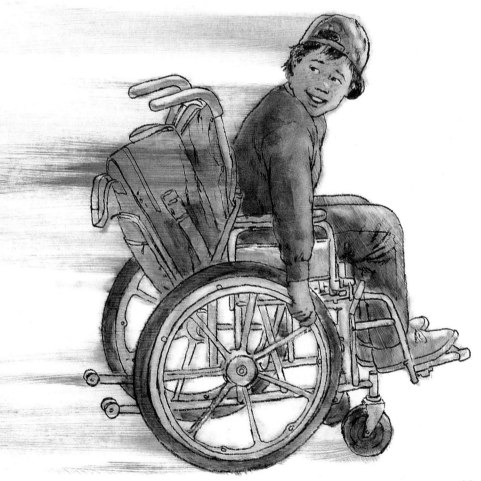

I use stairs.

Josh rolls down ramps.

900-941

22

And some things are easier
for me than for him.

But we both play Frisbee,

and we both like to swim.

We both love computers,

and we join the same clubs.

So as far as I can see,
Josh is a lot like me . . .

and just a *little* different.

WORD LIST

a	for	love	some
and	friend	loves	stairs
are	Frisbee	me	swim
as	he	monster	than
best	he's	movies	that's
both	him	music	the
but	I	my	things
can	is	of	this
catch	join	play	to
clubs	Josh	plays	use
computers	just	ramps	very
course	like	rolls	walk
different	listen	same	we
down	little	school	why
easier	lot	see	zooms
far		so	

About the Author

Bonnie Dobkin grew up with the last name Bierman in Morton Grove, Illinois. She attended Maine East High School and later received a degree in education from the University of Illinois. A high-school teacher for several years, Bonnie eventually moved into educational publishing and now works as an executive editor. She lives in Arlington Heights, Illinois.

For story ideas, Bonnie relies on her three sons, Bryan, Michael, and Kevin; her husband Jeff, a dentist; and Kelsey, a confused dog of extremely mixed heritage. When not writing, Bonnie focuses on her other interests—music, community theater, and chocolate.

About the Artist

Keith Neely attended the School of the Art Institute of Chicago and received a Bachelor of Fine Arts degree with honors from the Art Center College of Design, where he majored in illustration. He has worked as an art director, designer, and illustrator and has taught advertising illustration and advertising design at Biola College in La Mirada, California. Mr. Neely is currently a freelance illustrator whose work has appeared in numerous magazines, books, and advertisements. He lives in Los Osos, California, with his wife and five children.